Defoe
Abbott
Marx
Hardy
Melville
Machiavelli
Montaigne
Chesterton
Cooper
Emerson
Joyce
Austen
Hugo
Eliot
Grimm
Stoker
Carroll
Christie
Haggard
Molière
Byron
Schiller
Wilde
Maupassant
Engels
Garnett
Fitzgerald
Einstein
Hawthorne
Smith
Kafka
Goethe
Dostoyevsky
Cotton
Kipling
Doyle
Hall
Willis
Baum
Henry
Nietzsche
Leslie
Dumas
Flaubert
Turgenev
Balzac
Stockton
Vatsyayana
Crane
Burroughs
Verne
Curtis
Tocqueville
Gogol
Vinci
Homer
Widger
Tolstoy
Whitman
Busch
Darwin
Thoreau
Twain
Scott
Plato
Harte
Potter
Freud
Zola
Lawrence
Dickens
Burton
Hesse
Kant
Jowett
Stevenson
Andersen
Cervantes
Voltaire
London
Descartes
Poe
Aristotle
Wells
Burton
Cooke
Hale
James
Hastings
Bunner
Shakespeare
Irving
Richter
Chekhov
Chambers
da
Doré
Dante
Shaw
Benedict
Alcott
Swift
Wodehouse
Pushkin
Newton

tredition

tredition was established in 2006 by Sandra Latusseck and Soenke Schulz. Based in Hamburg, Germany, tredition offers publishing solutions to authors and publishing houses, combined with worldwide distribution of printed and digital book content. tredition is uniquely positioned to enable authors and publishing houses to create books on their own terms and without conventional manufacturing risks.

For more information please visit: www.tredition.com

TREDITION CLASSICS

This book is part of the TREDITION CLASSICS series. The creators of this series are united by passion for literature and driven by the intention of making all public domain books available in printed format again - worldwide. Most TREDITION CLASSICS titles have been out of print and off the bookstore shelves for decades. At tredition we believe that a great book never goes out of style and that its value is eternal. Several mostly non-profit literature projects provide content to tredition. To support their good work, tredition donates a portion of the proceeds from each sold copy. As a reader of a TREDITION CLASSICS book, you support our mission to save many of the amazing works of world literature from oblivion. See all available books at www.tredition.com.

Project Gutenberg

The content for this book has been graciously provided by Project Gutenberg. Project Gutenberg is a non-profit organization founded by Michael Hart in 1971 at the University of Illinois. The mission of Project Gutenberg is simple: To encourage the creation and distribution of eBooks. Project Gutenberg is the first and largest collection of public domain eBooks.

The Singing Mouse Stories

Emerson Hough

Imprint

This book is part of TREDITION CLASSICS

Author: Emerson Hough
Cover design: Buchgut, Berlin – Germany

Publisher: tredition GmbH, Hamburg - Germany
ISBN: 978-3-8472-2884-4

www.tredition.com
www.tredition.de

Copyright:
The content of this book is sourced from the public domain.

The intention of the TREDITION CLASSICS series is to make world literature in the public domain available in printed format. Literary enthusiasts and organizations, such as Project Gutenberg, worldwide have scanned and digitally edited the original texts. tredition has subsequently formatted and redesigned the content into a modern reading layout. Therefore, we cannot guarantee the exact reproduction of the original format of a particular historic edition. Please also note that no modifications have been made to the spelling, therefore it may differ from the orthography used today.

The Singing Mouse Stories

Emerson Hough

THE SINGING MOUSE STORIES

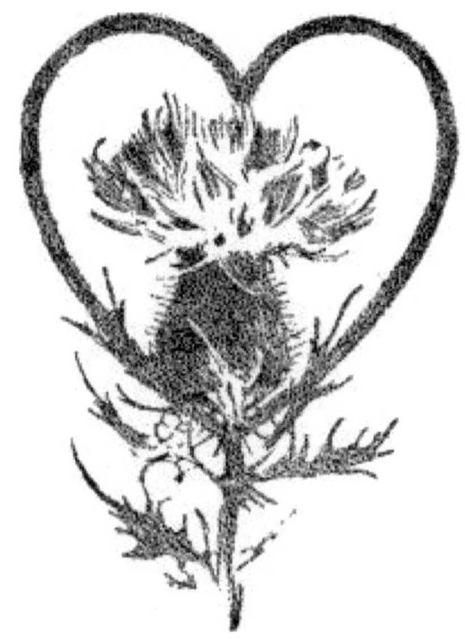

The Singing Mouse Stories

By
EMERSON HOUGH

With Decorations by

Mayo Bunker

CONTENTS

THE SINGING MOUSE STORIES

13 Thumbnail

The Land of the
Singing Mouse

T

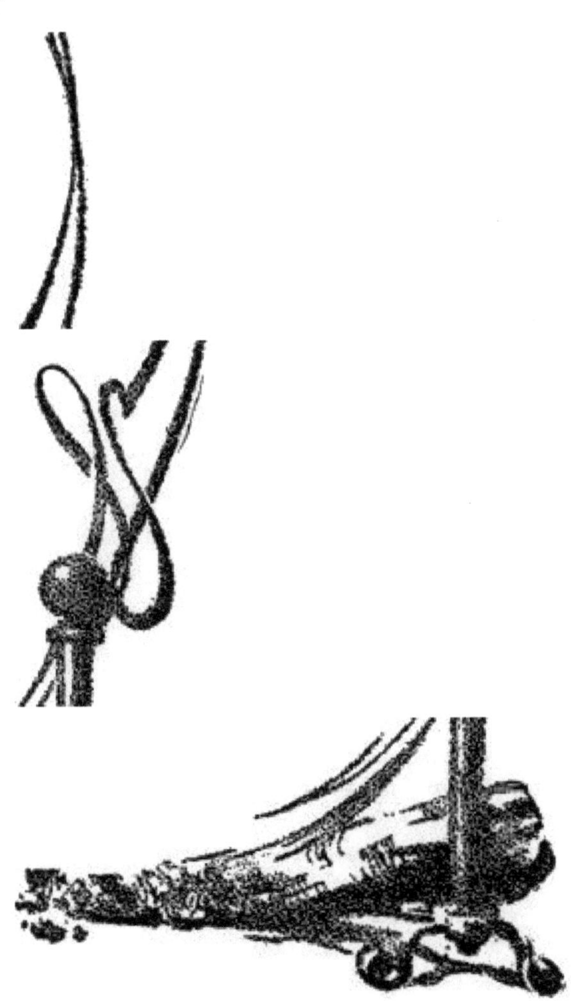

his is my room. I live here; and my friends come here sometimes, such as I have left. There is little to offer them, but they are welcome to what there is. There is the table. There is the fire. There are not any keys.

That is my coat upon the wall. It is worn, a little. The barrels of the old gun are worn; and the stock of the rifle, broken in the mountains long ago, is mended but rudely; and the tip of the old rod is broken, and the silk is fraying in the lashings, and upon the hand-grasp the cord is loose. The silver cord will loosen and break in the best of men in time; wherefore, I beseech you, mock 14 not at these belongings, though your own may far surpass them. You are welcome to anything there is here....

But the Singing Mouse will not come out, not while you are here. True, after you have gone, after the fire has burned down and the room is all still — usually near midnight, as I sit and muse alone over the dead or dying fire — true, then the Singing Mouse comes out and asks for its bit of bread; and then it folds its tiny paws and sits up, and turning its bright red eye upon me, half in power and half in beseeching, as of some fading memory of the past — why, it sings, I say to you; it sings! And I listen.... During such singing the fire blazes up. The walls are rich in art. My rod is new and trig. There is work, but there is no worry.... I am rich, rich! I have the Singing Mouse. And so 15 strange, so wondrous, so real are the things it sings; so bewitching is the song, so sweeter than that of any siren's; so broad and fine are the countries; so strong and true are the friendships; so brave and kind are the men I meet — so beautiful the whole world of the Singing Mouse, that when it is over, and in a chill I start up, I scarce can bear the shrinking in of the walls, and the grayness of the once red fire, and my gold turned to earthenware, and my pictures turned to splotches. In my hand everything I touch feels awkward. A pen — a pen — to talk of that? If one could use it while in the land of the Singing Mouse — then it might do. I think the pens there are not of wood and iron, stiff things of torture to reader and writer. I have a notion — though I have not examined the pens there — that they are made from plumes of an angel's 16 wing; and that if they chose they could talk, and say things which would make you and me ashamed and afraid. Pens such as these we do not have.

19

21 Thumbnail

The Burden
of a Song

T

he Singing Mouse came out. Quaintly and sweetly and with wondrous clearness it began an old, old song I first heard long ago. And as it sang, back with red electric thrill came the fine blood of youth, and beat in pulse with the song:

"When all the world is young, lad,

And all the trees are green,

And every goose a swan, lad,

And every lass a queen.

"Then hey! for boot and saddle, lad,

And round the world away!

Young blood must have its course, lad,

And every dog his day!"

22 And young blood began its course anew. Booted and spurred, into the saddle again! Face toward the West! And off for round the world away!

"There are green fields in Thrace," sighs the gladiator as he dies. And here were green fields in the land before us. Only, these were the inimitable and illimitable fields of Nature. Sheets and waves and billows and tumbles of green; oceans unswum, continents untracked, of thousandfold green. Then, on beyond, the gray, the gray-brown, the purple-gray of the higher plains; nearer than that, a broad slash of great golden yellow, a band of the sturdy prairie sunflowers; and nearer than that, swimming on the surface of the mysterious wave which constantly passes but is never past on the prairies, bright red roses, and strong larkspur, and at the bottom of this ever-shifting 23 sea, jewels in God's best blue enamel. You can not find this enamel in the windows. One must send for it to the land of the unswum sea.

A little higher and stronger piped the compelling melody. Why, here are the mountains! God bless them! Nay, brother, God has blessed them; blessed them with unbounded calm, with boundless strength, with unspeakable peace. You can take your troubles to the mountains. If you are Pueblo, Aztec, you can select some big mountain and pray to it, as its top shows the red sentience of the oncoming day. You can take your troubles to the sea; but the sea has troubles of its own, and frets. There is commerce on the sea, and the people who live near it are fretful, greedy, grasping. The mountains have no troubles; they have 24 no commerce. The dwellers of the mountains are calm and unfretted.

And on the broad shoulders of the mountains once more was cast the burden of the young man's troubles, and once more he walked deep into the peace of the big hills. And the mountains smiled not, neither wept, but gravely and kindly folded over, about, behind, the gray mantle of the cañon walls, and locked fast doors of adamant against all following, and swept a pitying hand of shadow, and breathed that wondrous unsyllabled voice of comfort which any mountain-goer knows. Ay! the goodness of such strength! Up by the clean snow; over the big rocks; by the lace-work stream where the trout are—why, it's all come again! That was the clink made by a passing deer. That was the touch of the green balsam—smell it, now! And there comes the mist, folding down the top; and there is the crash of the thunder; and this is the rush of the rain; and this is the warm yellow sun over it all—O, Singing Mouse, Singing Mouse!...

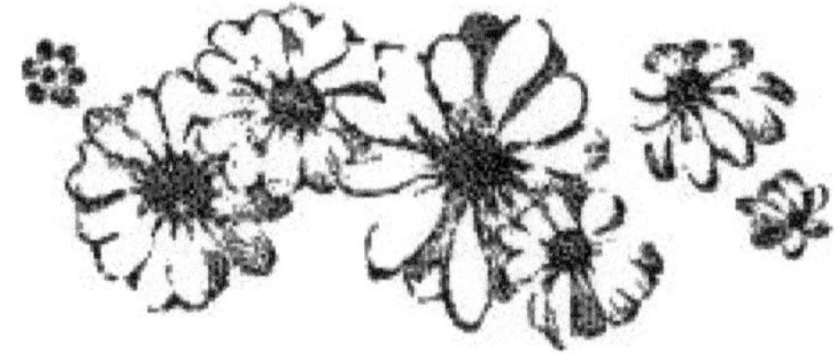

Back again, now, by some impulse of the dog which hasn't had any day. It is winter now, I remember, Singing Mouse, and I am walking by the shore of the great Inland Seas. There is snow on the ground. The trees look black in contrast as you gaze up from the beach against the high bank. It is cold. It is dark. There is a shiver in the air. There are icicles in the sky. Something is flying through the trees, but silent as if it came out of a grave. I have been walking, I know. I have walked a million miles, and I'm tired. My legs are stiff, and my legging has frozen fast to my overshoe; I remember that. And so I sit down—right here, you know—and look out over the lake—just over there, you see. The ice reaches out from the shore into the lake a long way; and it is covered with snow, and looks white. I can follow that white glimmer in a long, long curve to the right—twenty miles or more, maybe. Yes, it is cold. But ah! what is that out there, and what is it doing? It is setting all the long white curves of ice afire. It is throwing down hammered silver in a broad path, out there on the water. Those are not ripples. That is silver!

There will be angels walking on that pathway before long! That is not the moon coming up over the lake! It is the swinging open, by some careless angel's mischance, of the door of the White City of Rest!...

How old, how sore a man climbed up 27 the steep bank! There were white fields. In the distance a dog barked. Away across the fields a bright and cheery light shone out from a window, and as the moon rose higher, it showed the house which held the light. It was not a large house, but it seemed to be a home. Home!—what is that? I wondered; and I remember that I pulled at the frozen legging, and moved, with pain, the limbs grown tired and sore. And, as one looked at that twinkling, comfortable light, how plainly the rest of the old song came back:

"When all the world is old, lad,

And all the trees are brown,

And all the sports are stale, lad,

And all the wheels run down,

"Creep home and take your place there,

The sick and maimed among.

God grant you find one face there,

You loved when you were young."

28 The light in the little house went out. I think it was a happy home. May yours be so, always.

31

33 Thumbnail

The Little
River

The Singing Mouse came out and sat upon my knee. It fixed its
small red eye upon me, and lifted its tiny paws, so thin the fire
shone through them. And it sang.... Like the voice of some night-
wandering bird of melody, hid high in the upper realms of dark-
ness, came faint sweet notes falling softly down. It was as if from
the deep air above, and from the wide air around, there were
dropping and drifting small links of silken steel, gentle but strong,
so that one were helpless even had one wished to move. To listen
was also to see.

34 There were low rolling hills, covered and crowned with a
thick growth of hazel thickets and short oaks. Between these hills
ran long strips of green, strung on tiny bands of silver. And as
these bands moved and thickened and braided themselves together, I seemed to see a procession of the trees. The cottonwoods halt-
ed in their march. The box-elders, and maples, and water-elms,
and walnuts and such big trees swept grandly in with waving
banners, and wound on and on in long procession, even down to
two blue distant hills set at the edge of the world, unpassed guard-
ians of a land of dreams. Ah, well-a-day! I look back at those two
hills now, and the land of dreams lies still beyond them, it is true;
but it is now upon the side whence I first gazed. It is back there,
where one can not go again; back there, along that 35 crystal,
murmuring mystery of the little stream one knew when one was
young!

Ah, little river, little river, but I am coming back again. Once more
I push away the long grass and the swinging boughs, and look into

your face. Again I dabble my bare feet, and scoop up my straw hat full, and watch the tiny streams run down. Again I stand, bare and small and trembling, wondering if I can swim across. And—listen, little river—again at the same old place I shall cut me the willow wand, and down the long slope to the certain place I knew I am going to hurry, running the last quarter of a mile in sheer expectation, but forgetting not the binding on of the tough linen line. And now I cast my gaudy float on that same swinging, wimpling, dimpling eddy, and let it swim in beneath the bank. And—No! Can it 36 be? Have I here, now, again, plainly in my hands, the strange and wonderful creature, the gift of the little stream? Is this its form, utterly lovable? Is this its coat, wrought of cloth of gold and silver? Are these diamonds its eyes?... Oh, little river, little river, give me back this gift to keep for ever! Why take such things from us?... All I have I will give to you, if you will but give back to me, to have by me all the time, this little fish from the pool beneath the boughs. I have hunted well for him, believe me, hard and faithfully in many a place, but he is no longer there. I find him no longer, even in the remotest spots I search.... But this is he! This, in my hands, here in actual sight, is my first, my glorious, iridescent, radiant prize! Pray you, behold the glittering!

But along this little river there were 37 other things when the leaves grew brown. In those low, easy hills strange creatures dwelt. Birds of brown plumage and wondrous, soul-startling burst of wing. Large gray creatures, a foot long or longer, with light tread on the leaves, and long ears that went a-peak when you whistled to them. Were ever such beings before in any land? For the pursuit of these, it seems, one must have boots with copper toes, made waterproof by abundant tallow. There must be a vast game-bag—a world too large for a boyish form—and strange things to eat therein, such as one sees no longer; for on a chase calling for such daring-do it may be needful that one walk far, across the hills, along the little river, almost to the Delectable Mountains themselves. Again I see it all. Again I follow through the hills that same tall, tireless figure with 38 the grave and kindly face. Again I wonder at the uncomprehended skill which brought whirling down ten out of the dozen of those brown lightning balls. Again I rejoice, beyond all count or measure, over the first leporine murder committed by myself, the same furthered by means of a rest on a forked tree. It seems to me I groan secretly again at the weight of that great gun before the night has come. I almost wince again at the pulling off of those copper-toed boots at night, there by the kitchen stove, after the chase is done. But, ah! how happy I am again, holding up for the gaze of a kind pair of eyes this great, gray creature with the lopping ears.

Now, as we walk by the banks of this magic river, I would that it might be always as it was in the earliest days. I 39 like best to think myself mistaken when I suspect a greater stoop in this once familiar form which knew these hills and woods so well. It can not be that the quick eye has grown less bright. Yet why was the last mallard missed? And tell me, is not the old dog ranging as widely as once he did? Can it be that he keeps closer at heel? Does he look up once in a while, mournfully, with a dimmer eye, at an eye becoming also dimmer—does he walk more slowly, by a step now not so fast? Does he look up—My God!—is there melancholy in a dog's eye, too?

41

43 Thumbnail

What the
Waters Said

The fire was flickering fitfully and painting ghostly shadows on the wall. It was winter, and late in winter; indeed, the season was now at length drawing near to the end of winter, and approaching that dear time of spring which, beyond doubt, will be the eventful front and closing of the circle in the land where winter will not come.

I had drawn the little pine table close to the heap of failing embers, and aided by what light the sulky candle gave, was bending over and trying to arrange a patch on my old hunting-coat. It was an old, old hunting-coat, far gone in the sere and yellow leaf. It was old-fashioned 44 now, though once of proper cut and comeliness. It was disfigured, stained and worn. The pockets were torn down. The bindings were worn out. It was quite willing to be left alone now, hung by upon a forgotten nail, and subject to no further requisition. Nevertheless, if its owner wished, it could still do a day or two. I knew that; and something in the sturdy texture of its oft-tried nature excited more than half my admiration, and all my love.

Walpurgis on the ceiling, gray coming on in the embers, symptoms of death in the candle, a blotch of tallow on the Shakespeare, and the coat not half done. It must have been about then, I think, that the thin-edged sweetness of the Singing Mouse's voice pierced keenly through the air. I was right glad when the little creature came and sat on my 45 knee, and in its affectionate way began to nibble at my finger-tips. It sat erect, its thin paws waving with a tiny, measured swing, and in its mystic voice, so infinitely small, so sweet and yet so majestically strong, began a song which no pen can transcribe. Knowing that the awakening must come, but unwilling to lose a moment of the dream, I, who with one finger could have crushed the little thing, sat prizing it more and more, as more and more its voice swept, and swelled, and rang; rang, till the fire burst high in noble pyramids of flame; rang, till the candle flashed in a thousand crystals; swelled, till the walls fell silently apart, and showed that all this time I had been sitting ignorant of, but yet within a grand and stately hall, whose polished sides bore speaking canvas and noble marbles; swept up and around, till 46 every stately niche, and every tapestried corner, and every lofty dome rang gently back in mellow music—all for the Singing Mouse and me....

Small wizard, it was fell cunning of ye so to paint upon the wall this picture of the old mill-dam. How naturally the wooded hill slopes back beyond the mill! And how, with the same old sleepy curves, the river winds on back. How green the trees—how very green! Ah, Singing Mouse, they do not mix that color now. And nowhere do wide bottom-lands wave and sing in such seemly grace, so decked with yellow flowers, with odd sweet william and the small wild rose. And nowhere now on earth, I know, is there any stream to murmur so sweetly and so comfortably, to say such words to any dreaming boy, to babble of a work 47 well done, of conscience clear and of a success and happiness to come. All that was in the river. If I listen very hard, and imagine very high and very deep, I can almost pretend to hear them now, those old words, heard when I was young. The voices are there, I doubt not, and there are other boys. God keep them boys always, and may they dream not backward, but ahead!

This lazy pool beneath the far wing of the dam, how smooth it looks! Yet well we know the sunken log upon its farther side. We have festooned it full oft with a big hook and hempen line. And from that pool how many fatuous fishes have we not hauled forth. Here we came often, when we were boys; and once did not certain bold souls sleep here all night, curled up along the bank, waking the 48 next morning, each with a sore throat, 'tis true, but with heart full proud at such high deed of valor!

And there is the long wooden bridge. What a feat of engineering that bridge once seemed to our untraveled souls! Behold it now, as it was then, lying in the level rays of the rising moon, a brilliant causeway leading over into a land of mystery, to glory, perhaps; perhaps to failure, forgetfulness, oblivion and rest. And there, I declare, at the other end of this great roadway — swimming up, I declare, in the same old way — is the great round moon whose light served us when we stayed late at the dam in the summer evenings. And the shadows of the bridge timbers are just as long and black; and the ripples over the rocks at the middle span are just as beautiful and white. And here, right at our feet again, 49 the moon is playing its old tricks of painting faces in the water....

There are too many faces in the water, Singing Mouse; and I beg you, cease repeating the words about the *Corpus Delicti*! You would make one shudder. Let us look no more at the faces in the water.

But still you bide by the waters tonight, wizard; for here is a picture of the sea. It is the sea, and it is talking, as it always does. There are some who think the sea speaks only of sorrow, but this is not wholly true. If you will listen thoughtfully enough, you will find that it is not all of troubles that the sea is whispering. Nor does it speak always of restlessness and change. Some find a stimulus beside the sea, and say it brings forgetfulness. Rather let us call it exaltation. 50 Much more than of a petty excitement, fit to blot a man's momentary woes, it speaks in a sterner and a stronger note. It throbs with the pulse of a further shore. It speaks of a quiet tide making out to the Fortunate Islands, and tells of a way of following gales, and of a new Atlantis, somewhere on beyond. How dear this dream of a different land, this story of Atlantis, pathetically sought! Certainly, Atlantis is there, out beyond, somewhere in the sea; and truly there are those who have discovered it, and those who still may do so. I know it, Singing Mouse, for I can read it written in the hollow of this tiny shell of pink you have found here by the shore — borne across to us, we may not doubt, by an understanding tide from a place happily attained by those who wrote the message and sought to let us know.

51

"Long time upon the mast our brown sail flapped;

Our keel plowed bitter salt, and everywhere

The ominous sky in sullen mystery wrapped,

What side we looked on, either here or there,

The welcome sight of land long sadly sought;

And that Atlantis, hid within the sea,

The land with all our hope and promise fraught,

We saw not yet, nor wist where it might be.

"But as we sailed as manful as we might,

And counted not the sail more fit than oar,

Lo! o'er the wave there burst a vision bright

Of wood, and winding stream, and easy shore.

Then by the lofty light which shone above,

We knew at last our voyage sad was o'er,

52

And we hard by the haven for which we strove,

And soon all past the need to wander more.

"Then as our craft made safely on the strand,

And we all well our weary brown sail furled,

We gazed as strangers might at that fair land,

And hardly knew if it might be our world;

Till One took gently every weary hand,

And led us on to where still waters be,

And whispered softly, 'Lo! it hath been planned

That thou at last this pleasant place shouldst see.'

"And as those dreaming so awakened we,

And looked with eyes unhurt on that fair sky,

And whispered, hand in hand and eye to eye,

"Tis our Atlantis, risen from the sea —

'Tis our Atlantis, from the bitten sea!

'Tis our Atlantis, come again, oh, friend, to thee and me!'"

55

57 Thumbnail

Lake

Belle-Marie

Lake Belle-Marie lies far away. Beyond the forest the mountains are white. Beyond the mountains the sky rises blue, high up into the infinite Unknown.

I do not know where the Singing Mouse lives. No man can tell what journeys it may make such times as it is absent from the room that holds the pine table, and the book, and the candle, and the open fire. But last night when the faint, shrill sweetness of its little voice grew apart from the lonely silence of the room, and I turned and saw the Singing Mouse sitting on the corner of the book, the light of the candle shining pink 58 through its tiny paws, almost the first word it said was of the far-off Lake of Belle-Marie.

"Do you see it?" asked the Singing Mouse.

"You mean—"

"The moon there through the window? Do you see the moon and the stars? Do you know where they are shining to-night? Do you see them, there, deep in the water? Do you know where that is? Do you know the water? I know. It is Lake Belle-Marie."

And all I could do was to sit speechless. For the fire was gone, and the wall was open, and the room was not a room. The voice of the Singing Mouse, shrill and sweet, droned on a thousand miles away in smallness, but every word a crystal of regret and joy.

"A thousand feet deep, or more, or 59 bottomless, lies Lake Belle-Marie, for no man has ever fathomed it. But no matter how deep, the moon lies to-night at the bottom, and you can see it shining there, deep down in the blue. The stars are smaller, so they stay up and sparkle on the surface. The forest is very black to-night, is it not? and the shadow of the pines on the point looks like a mass of actual substance. Wait! Did you see that silver creature leap from the quiet water? You may know the shadow is but a shadow, for you can see the chasing ripples pass through it and break it up into a crinkled fabric of the night.

"Do you see the pines waving, away up there in their tops, and do you hear them talking? They are always talking. To-night they are saying: 'Hush, Belle-Marie; slumber, Belle-Marie; we will watch, we will watch, hush, hush, hush!' 60 Didn't you ever know what the pines said? They wish no one ever to come near Lake Belle-Marie. Well for you that you only sat and looked at the face of Belle-Marie, and cast no line nor fired untimely shot around such shores! The pines would have been angry and would have crushed you. You do not know how they live, seeking only to keep Belle-Marie from the world, standing close and sturdy together and threatening any who approach. It would break their hearts to have her hiding-place found out. You do not know how they love her. The pines are old, old, old, many of them, but they told me that no footprint of man was ever seen upon those shores, that no boat ever rested on that little sea, neither did ever a treacherous line wrinkle even the smallest portion of its smoothest coves. Believe me, to have 61 Belle-Marie known would break the hearts of the pines. They told me they lived all the time only that they might every night sing Belle-Marie to sleep, and every morning look upon her face, innocent, pure, unknown and unknowing, therefore good, sincere and utterly trustworthy. That is why the pines live. That is what they are talking about. In many places I know the hearts of the pines are broken, and they grieve continually. That is because there are too many people. In this valley the pines do not grieve. They only talk among themselves. In the morning they will wave their hands quite gaily and will say: 'Waken, waken, Belle-Marie! Sweet is the day, sweet is the day, God hath given, given, given!' That is what the pines say in the morning.

"The white mountains yonder are very 62 old. How strong and quiet they are, and how sure of themselves! To be quiet and strong one needs to be old, for small things do not matter then. Do you know what the mountains think, as they stand there shoulder to shoulder — for they live only to shield and protect the forest, here in the valley. They told me they were thinking of the smallness and the quickness of the days. 'Age unto age!' is what the mountains whisper. 'Æon unto æon! Strong, strong, strong is Time!'

"And yet I knew these mighty pillars stood only to shield the forest which shielded Belle-Marie. So I stood upon the last mountain and looked upon the great blue of the sky, and there again I saw the face of Lake Belle-Marie; and the circle was complete, and I sought no more, for I knew that from the abode of 63 perfect, unhurt nature it is but a step up to the perfect peace and rest of the land where lives that Time whose name the mountains voice in awe.

"And now, do you see what is happening on Lake Belle-Marie? Through the cleft in the forest the pink of the early day is showing, and light shines through the spaces of the pines. And down the pebbles of the beach, knee-deep into the shining flood, steps a noble creature, antlered, beautiful, admirable. Do you see him drink, and do you see him raise his head and look about with gentle and fearless eye? This creature is of the place, and no hand must harm him.

"Let the thin, blue smoke die down. Attempt no foot farther on. Disturb not this spot. Return. But before you go, take one more look upon the Lake of Belle-Marie!"

64 So again I gazed upon the face of the lake, which seemed innocent, and sincere, and trustworthy, and deserving of the protection of the league of the pines, and the army of the mountains, and the canopy of the unshamed sky. And then the voice of the Singing Mouse, employed in some song whose language I do not yet fully understand, faded and sank away; and even as it passed the walls came back and the ashes lay gray upon the hearth.

69 Thumbnail

The Skull and
the Rose

The Singing Mouse peeped out from the hollow orbit of the

white skull which lies upon the table next to the volume of Shakespeare. It reached down a tiny pink paw and touched a leaf of the brave red rose which every day lies before the skull. It plucked the leaf, which made a buckler for its small throbbing breast. It spoke:

"The rose is bold and red," said the Singing Mouse. "Blood is red. A skull is white. The rose and the skull love one another. They understand. We do not understand.

"As I sat by the skull I saw a dream 70 of the past go by. It was as you see it now.

"Do you see the waving grasses of the valleys? Do you see the unmoving front of the white old mountains? Do you see the red roses growing down among the grasses?

"It is peace upon the land. I can see one who has seen the lands. He smiles, but he is sad. He crosses the wide sea, but cares not. He travels upon rails of iron, and he smiles, but still is sad, because he thinks; and he who thinks must weep. He leaves the ship and the iron rail, and his road is narrower and slower, for he travels now by wheels of wood. He sees the valleys, and his smile has more of peace. His trail becomes narrower yet. He goes by saddle, and the mountains hem him in, but now he smiles the more. Now he must leave even the 71 saddle, and the trail is dim and hard. See, the trail is gone! Here, where no foot has trod, where the mountains close about, where the trees whisper, he sits and looks about him. Do you see the red rose on his breast? Always the rose is there. Do you see him look up at the mountains, about him at the trees? Do you see him lay his head upon the earth? Do you still see his smile, the smile which is weary and yet not afraid? Do you hear him sigh? And what is this he whispers, here at the end of the long and narrowing way—'I know not if this be the end or the beginning!' Ah, what does this man mean who whispers to himself in riddles?

"Look! It is the time of war. There is music. The blood stings. The heart leaps. The eye flames. The soul exults. Flickering of light on steel, the flash of 72 servant forces used to slay, the reverberant growl of engines made for death, the passing of men in cloth and men in blankets, the tramp of hurrying hoofs, the falling of men who die—can you see this—can you catch the horror, the exultation, the joy of this, I say? They come, they go; they run their race, and it is all.

"Here are those who ride against those who slay. Do you know this one who rides at the head, smiling, swinging his sword well and smiling all the time? It is he who said in the mountains that riddle of the end and the beginning—who knew that to the heart of nature we must come, for either the end or the beginning of this, our life. Do you see upon his breast the red rose? I think he rides to battle with the rose, knowing what fate will come.

73 "You know of this biting whistle in the air—this small thing that smites unseen? Do you know the mowing of the death scythes? Hark! I hear the singing of this unseen thing. See! he of the rose is bitten. He has fallen. Ay! ay! He was so brave and strong! His horse has gone. He is alone. The grass here was so green. It is red. The rose upon his breast is red. His face is white, but still the smile is there; and now it is calmer and more sweet, though still he whispers, 'I know not if it be the end or the beginning!'

"He is alone with Nature again. The heavens weep for him. The grasses and leaves begin with busy fingers to cover him up. The earth pillows him. He sleeps. It is all. It is done. It is the way of life. It is the end and the beginning.

"He loved the valley, the mountain, 74 the grass, the rose. Now, since he cherished the rose so well, see, the rose will not leave him. Out of the dust it rises, it grows, it blooms. Against his lips it presses. It is the beginning! He loved, he thought, he knew. He is not dead He is with Nature. It is but the beginning!

"Let the rose press against his lips in an eternal, pure caress. There is no end. They understand. We do not yet understand."

The pink flame of the unreal light died away. The pageant of the hills, the panorama of the battle, faded and were gone. The table and the books came back. Wondering at these words, I scarce could tell when the Singing Mouse went away, leaving me staring at the barren walls and at the white skull by my hand. 75 ... For a moment it nearly seemed to me the hollow eyes had light and spoke to me. For a moment almost it seemed to me that the rose stirred deep down among its petals, and that a wider perfume floated out upon the air.

77

The Man of the
Mountain

The Man of the Mountain

"Once there was a man," said the Singing Mouse, "who loved to go into the mountains. He would go alone, far into the mountains, and climb up to the tops of the tallest peaks. Nothing pleased him so much as to climb to the top of some mountain where no other man had ever been. No one ever knew what he said to the mountains, or what the mountains said to him, but that they understood each other very well was sure, for he could go among the mountains where other men dared not go. At the tops of the high mountains he would sit and look out over the country that lay beyond.

He would not say what he saw, 80 for he said he could not tell, and that, moreover, the people would not understand it, for they did not know the way the mountains thought.

"One time this man climbed to the top of a very high mountain peak in a distant country. This peak looked out over a wide land, and the man knew that from its summit he could see many things.

"The man was now growing old, so when he got to the top of this mountain he sat down to rest. When he sat down, he put his chin in his hand, and his arm upon his knee; and so he looked out over the land, seeing many things.

"The sun came up, but the man did not move, but sat and thought. The moon came, but still he did not move. He only looked, and thought and smiled.

"After many days it was seen that this man would not come down from the 81 mountain. The mountain made him part of itself, and turned him into stone, as he sat there, with his chin in his hand. He is there to-day, looking out over many things. He never moves, for he is now of stone. I have seen that place myself. Once I thought I heard this man whisper of the things he saw. He sits there to-day."

83

85 Thumbnail

At the Place
of the Oaks

"Do you know what the oak says?" asked the Singing Mouse,
as it sat upon my knee. It had needed to nibble again at my fin-

gers before it could waken me from the dream into which I had fallen, gazing at the fading fire. "Do you know what the oak says?" it repeated. "Do you hear it? Do you hear the talking of the leaves?...

"I know what the oak says," said the Singing Mouse. "When the wind is soft, the oak says: 'Peace! Peace!' When the breeze is sharp it sighs and says: 'Pity! Pity! Pity!' And when the storm has fallen, the oak sobs and cries: 'Woe! Woe! Woe.'

86 "Do you see the oaks?" asked the Singing Mouse. "Do you see the little lake? Do you know this place of the oaks? Behold it now!" It waved a tiny hand.

I gazed at the naked, cheerless wall, seamed and rent with cracks along its sallow width. And as I gazed the seams and scars blended and composed into the lines of a map of a noble country. And as I gazed more intently the map took on color, and narrowed its semblance to that of a certain region. And as I gazed yet more eagerly the map faded quite away, and there lay in its stead the smiling face of an enchanted land.

There was the little silver lake, rippling on its shore of rushes. Around rose the long curved hills, swelling back from the shore. The baby river babbled on at 87 the mouth of the lake, kissing its mother a continual farewell. The small springs tinkled metallically cold into the silver of the lake. The tender green of the gentle glades rolled softly back, dividing the two hills in peaceful separation. And there were the oaks. At the water's edge, near the lesser spring, the wild apple trees twisted, but upon the hills and over the great glades stood the reserved, mysterious oaks, tall and strong.

One oak, a mighty one, now resolved itself more prominently forth. Did I not know it well? Could one forget the tortured but noble soul of this oak? Could one forget the strong arm of comfort it extended over this most precious spot of all the glade? One must suffer before one may comfort. The oak had suffered somewhere. We do not know all things. But over this spot the great tree reached 88 out sheltering hands, and certainly from its hands dropped benedictions plenteously down.

Under the arm of the oak I saw a tiny house of white—neat, well-ordered, full of cheerfulness. Through the wall of canvas—for it now seemed to be after dusk—there shone a faint pink gleam of light, the soul of the white house, its pure spirit of content. As it shone, it scarce seemed lit by mortal hand.

Near the small house of white, and under the oak's protecting arm, there burned a little flame, of small compass save in the vast shadows it set dancing among the trees. Those who built this fire here, so many times, so many years, each time first craved pardon of the green grass of that happy glade, for they would not harm the grass. But the grass said yea to all they asked, this was sure, for 89 each year the tiny hearth spot was greener than any other spot, because it remembered what the fire had said and done. And each year the oak dropped down food enough for the little fire. The oak took pay in the vast shadows the fire made for it. That was the way the oak saw the spirits of the Past, and when it saw them it sighed; but still it welcomed the shadows of the Past. So the fire, and the grass, and the oak, and the shadows of the Past were friends, and each year they met here. It had been thus for many years. Each year, for many years, the same hand had laid the little fire, in the same place, and so given back to the oak its Past. Now, the Past is a very sad but tender thing.

Near by the little fire I saw a small table formed of straight-laid boughs, and at either side of this were seats made cunningly 90 in the workshop of the woods. There were two forms at this small table. I saw them both. One was gray and bowed somewhat, stooped as the oaks are, silvered as the oaks are in the winter days. The other was younger and more erect. Once the younger looked to the older for counsel, but now it seemed to me the bowed figure turned to the one that had become more strong.

I saw the savory vapors rise. Even, it seemed to me, I could note a faint, clear odor of innocent potency. I saw the table laid, not with gleam of snow and silver, but with plain vessels which, nevertheless, seemed now to have a radiance of their own. I knew all this. It was as though there actually lay at hand these pleasant scenes, as though there actually arose the appealing fragrance of the evening meal.

91 Now as I looked, the gray figure bowed its head, there, under the arm of the oak, and asked on the humble board the blessing of the God who made the oak, and gave the fire and spread the pleasant waters on the land. Every mealtime, every year, for many years, it had been thus. Ever, the oak knew, the gray figure would first bow and ask the blessing of God. And each time at the close the oak with rustling leaves pronounced distinct Amen! Let those jest who will. I do not know. I think perhaps the oak knows or it would not thus for years have whispered reverently its distinct Amen! I will not scoff. It is perhaps we who are ignorant. We do not know all things.

I ask not what nor who were these two who had come each year to this place of the oaks, but surely they were friends. 92 In shadow, I could hear them talk. In shadow, I could see them smile.

These friends sat by the little fire a time before they went to rest in the tiny house of white. After they had gone, the fire did strange things. All men know that, though you see the fire burned down, when you go into the tent you will some time in the night see the walls lit up by a sudden flash or so, now and then, from the fire which was thought to be dead.

That is the business of the fire, and of the oaks and of the shadows. I know that the shadows dance strangely, and hover and come near at hand, in those late hours of the night; but what then occurs I do not know. These two friends never questioned this. They knew it was the secret of the night, and gave the oak its own request, in pay for 93 its protection and consent. They gave the oak its union with the sacred Past.

In the night I have heard the oak sob. Yet in the morning, when the sun was silvering the wake of all the leaping fishes, the oak was always gentle, and it said, "Wake, wake! God is wise. Waken, waken! God is good!"

As pure shining beads upon a thread of gold I saw this small, dear picture, reiterant and unchanged, year after year, always with the same calm and pure surroundings. Only as year added itself to year, slipping forward on the golden string, I saw the gray figure grow more gray, more bowed, more feeble. Alas! it seemed to me I saw the silver coming upon the head of the younger man, and his eyes growing weary, as of one who looks at the earth too closely (which it is 94 not wise to do). Yet the years came, to the oaks and to the grasses and to the friends.

The grass dies every year, but it is born again. The oak dies in centuries, but it is born again. Man dies in three score years and ten; but he, too, is born again.

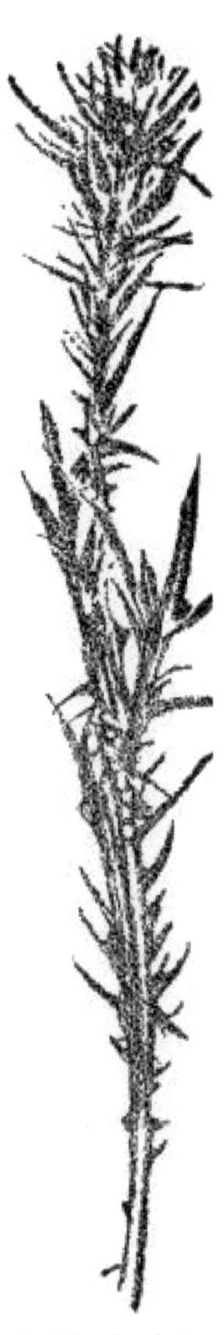

As I looked, I could see the passing of the years. In all but the un-
altering fire of friendship I could see change creeping on. Grayer,
grayer, more bent, more feeble—is it not so, Singing Mouse? And
now, this time, what was this gentle warning that the oak tried to

whisper softly down? Perhaps the grayer friend heard it, as he sat musing by the fire. He rose and looked about him, as one who had dreamed and was content. He looked up at the solemn stars unafraid, and so murmured to himself. "Day unto day 95 uttereth speech," he said; "Night unto night showeth knowledge."

Day unto day, Singing Mouse. Day unto day.

Woe is me, Singing Mouse, and these are bitter tears for that which you have shown I see it all again, the oaks, the glade, the tiny house of white, the small pleasant fire. Here again is the little table, and here is the evening meal. The table is still spread for two. A double portion is served as was wont before. Yet why? For all is not the same. At this table there is but one form now. The younger man is there, although now he has grown gray and stooped. Year unto year, day unto day, the beads have slipped along the string. Once young, now old, he keeps the camp alone!

But is he then alone? Hush! The 96 squirrels have grown still, and even the oak is silent. What is that opposite, across the table, at the seat long years held only by the elder of these two? Tell me, Singing Mouse, is it not true that I see there, sitting as of old at the table, the same sturdy form, the same simple, innocent and believing face? It is the gray ghost of one grown gray in goodness. It is the shadow of a shadow, the apparition of a soul!

The one at the table pauses, as was the wont before the beginning of a meal. He looks across the table to the shadow, as if the shadow were his friend. The shadow bows its head. The living man bows also his head at the board. The shadow moves its lips. Doubt not those words are heard this day.

See, the sun rises through the trees. The glorious day sets on once more. 97 Doubt not, fear not, sorrow not, ye two. Bow the head still, ye two, and let not my picture perish. Whisper again the benediction of the years, and let me hear once more the murmur of the oak's Amen!

101 Thumbnail

The Birth of
the Hours

"Do you know the story of the Wedding of the Times?" said the Singing Mouse. "You know, all life is a wedding. The flowers love, and the grasses, and the trees; and the circle of the wedding ring is the circle of life and the sign of eternity. Death and life, not life and then death, is the order and the law.

"The hours are born of parents, as are the flowers. The hours of the day are born of the wedding of Night and Morning. It is the way of Life. Come with me."

So with the Singing Mouse I went into a place where I was once long before. I could see it very well. It was in the deep 102 woods, far away. Near by there were tall, sweet grasses. I could hear the faint tinkle of a falling stream. Other than that, it was silent in the deep woods. Overhead the sky was clear and filled with stars. The stars trembled and twinkled and shone radiantly fair. So now all at once I knew they were the jewels on the veil of Night. And the far shadows were the drapery of the Night, and the greater light of the heavens was the star upon her coronal.

When I first looked forth, the Night was a babe, but as I gazed it grew. The Night is full of change and charm. Those who live within the walls do not see these things. When I saw them, I could not sleep, for the Night in all her changes seemed to speak.

The Night grew older, drawing about her her more ornate garb of witchery. 103 Across her bosom fell a wondrous tissue, trembling with exuberance of unprismed light. These were the gems in thousands of the skies, all fair against the blackness of the robes of Night, and I knew that the blackness of the one was as lovely as the radiance of the other. Nor could one separate one from the other, for there arose a thin mist of light, so that one saw form or features only dimly, as through a cloth of silver lace, such as the spiders weave upon a morning.

The Night grew on, changing at every moment, for change is the law. There were small frowns of clouds which were replaced by smiles of light. Did never you hear the laughter of the Night? It is a strange thing. Not all men have heard it. The Singing Mouse told me of this.

Now as I lay and looked at this glorious apparition, there came still another 104 change, and one most wonderful. In the heart of the Night there came a tremulous exultation. Upon the face of the Night appeared a roseate tinge of joyous perturbation. So then I knew the lover of the Night was coming, and knew, too, whence we have derived the signs of love as among human beings we see it indicated. I saw the flush upon the cheek of Night flame slowly and faintly up, until it touched her very forehead. This is the way of Love. But the Night went on, for this is the way of Life. Love and Life, these are ever and for ever. We mock at them and understand them not, but they are ever and for ever.

And now the Night, I know not whether startled or in joy, whether ashamed of her dark garb, or unconscious of it in the proud sureness of her beauty, dropped loose a portion of the 105 shadows of her robe, and stood forth radiant, clad with the dazzling beauty of her stars. Then she raised her hand and laid it on her heart.

And so the Morning came and took her in his arms and kissed her on the brow. So here was Love again. And of this wedding there were born the hours.

107

109

The Stone that
Had no Thought

"Once," said the Singing Mouse, "while many men hurried into the city, as, each day, they do, they saw many other men standing about a place where a large building was growing. There were those who raised stones on long arms of steel, and swung them about, high up into the wall. Others remained upon the earth to place these stones upon the long arms of steel. Now a stone had fallen, and beneath it lay what had been a man; and around this many stood.

"The long arm reached out after stones, and so this stone again was taken and raised into the air. That which had 110 been a man lay broken, never again to rise and smile and walk. Near to it stood a woman, not weeping, being still too sad for weeping. Above her arose the stone once more, heavy and without thought. It rose above the woman and above this that had been a man, and as it swung high and slow above her the woman looked up at it, as though to ask of it mercy. But the stone passed slowly on, heavy and without thought. It is in the wall to-day, heavy and without thought. Some say that is a temple, others that there is a God in it. But no God replies. And the stone is in the wall, heavy, without thought."

113

The Tear
and the Smile

The Tear
and the Smile

The Singing Mouse came and sat near by. Undoubtedly the room was dingy to the last degree. The dust lay thick upon the corner of the table. It crusted the window ledge and hung upon the sallow wall. What was the use, things being as they were, to disturb the dust? Let it lie in all its bitterness. And let the charred ends of the fagots roll out upon the floor. And let the fire die down to ashes. Dust to dust. Ashes to ashes. It was very fit.

But the Singing Mouse came and sat near by. I could hear it patter among the dead leaves of the flowers that lay upon the table. I turned my head and saw it 116 sitting close by my fallen hand. Its tiny paws were waving. I could see its breast, for which a rose leaf would have been a giant buckler, pulsing and beating above its throbbing heart. Its eyes were shining.... A rhythm came into the swing of the pink-tinted paws. And then, so high and thin and sweet that at first I looked above to trace the sound, there came the singing of the Singing Mouse.... Dreams fell upon my eyes.

I heard that sweet sound of the woods, the tinkle of falling water, which is so full of change, now keen, clear and metallically musical, now soft, slurred and full of sleep. I could not see the little stream, but knew it ran down there beneath the talking pines. But very well one could see the hill where the small white house had stood among the trees. The white house was gone now, though the grass 117 pressed down by the blankets had not yet fully arisen. The smoke of the camp-fire still wavered up. It followed one, with long, out-reaching arms of vapor. With its fingers it beckoned and begged for its old companions yet a while. Did never one look back at the smoke of the camp-fire that one leaves? Always, the heart of the fire will stir at this time of parting. A little blaze will burst out among the embers, and the smoke will reach out and beckon one to stay. It is very hard to leave such a fire.

Certainly there must be strange things, of which we know but little. Surely there was a figure in the wreath of smoke. I could see the drapery shape itself about a form. I could see the outstretched arms. I could see the face, the gravely smiling lips.

"There are many things in the land of 118 the Singing Mouse," murmured my small magician. "It is only there that one sees clearly." So I looked and listened to the figure which was in the smoke of the little fire.

"Believe me," said the figure in the smoke, "the ashes and the dust are not so bitter as you think them. The tears rain on them, and they go back into the earth and are born again. Look around you, as here you may look, unhindered by any confining walls. Do you not see the flowers smiling bravely? Yet every blossom is a tear. Do you not see the strong forest trees? Yet every tree grows on the ashes of the past. We know not what you mean by grief. With us, all things point to Hope. I have swum above a thousand forests. Ask this forest, the youngest of them all, whether it whispers of dread and of grief. Rather it 119 whispers of wonder and of joy. Come to it, and it may tell you of its comfort. Turn your eyes up to the blue sky, and put your hands out upon this grass, which is but dust renewed, and at your eyes and at your fingers you shall drink peace and knowledge. The shape of a room and of a grave is square and cruel, but the shape of the earth and of the great sky is that of the perpetual circle, and it is kind. Come to these. Come to me. I will wave my hands above you, and you shall sleep. When you awaken the flowers will be blooming; and upon the lid of each you shall see the tear, but upon the lips of each shall rest a smile."

So now the figure in the smoke waved, and nodded, and smiled and beckoned, until I said to the Singing Mouse it seemed scarce like things we ordinarily know.

120 "Lie down and sleep," said the Singing Mouse.

So I lay down and slept. And when I awoke there were some small flowers not far away; and when I looked I saw it was as had been said. Each flower had a tiny tear hidden away beneath its lid, but upon the lips of each there rested a brave smile. And from among the flowers there arose a sweet odor.

"This," said the Singing Mouse, when it saw me note the fragrance, "this is a Memory. It belongs to you. See how soft and sweet it is."

123

125 Thumbnail

**How the Mountains
Ate up the Plains**

"I once knew a man," said the Singing Mouse, "who had seen the mountains in the winter time, when they were covered deep in snow. It is the belief of most men that the mountains are then asleep, but this man said that they are not asleep, but that they have only drawn over their heads the white council-robes, for then they are sitting in council. Now the mountains are very old and wise. This man told me he heard strange sounds coming from under the council-robes of the mountains then, voices not distinctly heard, but wonderful 126 and strong and of a sort to make one fear.

"This man told me that once he heard the mountains tell of a time when they ate up the plains. 'Once man was a dweller of the plains,' sang the mountains in a great song; 'there man dug and strove. Never he lifted up the eye, but at his feet, at his feet, there he still gazed down. The clouds bore not up his gaze, neither did the hills comfort him. Things false, of no worth, these man sought and prized. Though we whispered to him, still he made deaf his ear. Then we, the mountains, we the strong, the just, the wise, we rose, we set together our shoulders and so marched on. Thus we ate up the plain. Now we stand where once man was, for man lifted not up his eyes. Therefore, now let man look up, let him not make small his gaze. We the 127 strong, we the just, the wise, we shall eat up the plain. For on our brows sits the light, about our heads is the calm. That which is high shall in the days prevail. We the strong, the just, the wise, this we have said!'

"This man told me that he could not hear all the song that the mountains chanted, nor all they whispered among themselves. But he thought they said that they had swallowed up and consumed one race of beings who became fixed only upon the winning of what they called wealth, and had crushed out this wealth and burned up their precious things. This may be true, for to-day men visit the mountains to dig there for wealth, and this which they call gold is found much scattered, as though it had been crumbled and burned and blown wide over the earth upon the four winds. 128 For these reasons this man thought that the mountains had once eaten up the plains; and that perhaps at some time they might do this again."

131

133 Thumbnail

The Savage and
Its Heart

"Once," said the Singing Mouse, "I knew a man who found a little dog, starved, beneath a building where it had been left. He took it and fed it; and each time he held out his hand to give it food, it bit his hand, knowing not that he was its friend. Many

times he fed it, and always it bit his hand. It was a long time before it learned that the man was its friend. It was but a savage. He
fed it patiently, and so after a time the dog bit him no more, having learned that he was its friend. When it had ceased to be savage, it loved him. The man gave it neither blow nor unkindness,
and fed it, knowing that he was older and more 134 wise and that
in time it might love him. So at last it did; and this may often
happen for those who wait, large and kind and patient; and so
often friends are made."

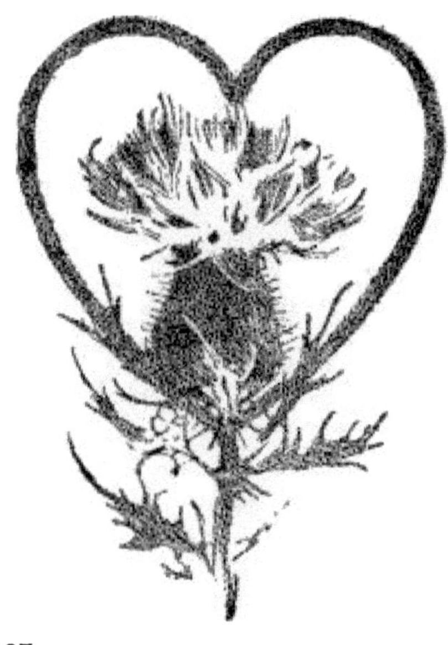

137

139 Thumbnail

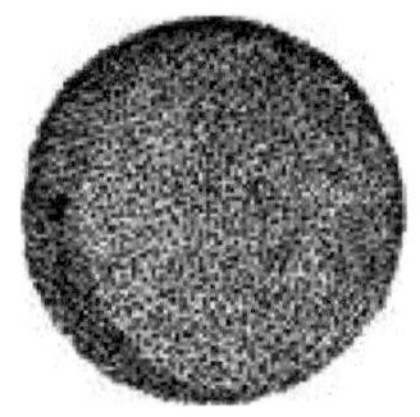

The Beast
Terrible

The little room was resplendent one night with a fire which flamed and flickered gloriously. It set in motion many shadows which had their home in the corners of the walls, and bade them cease their sullenness and come forth to dance in the riot of the hour. And so each shadow found its partner in a ray of firelight, and there they danced. They danced about the tangled front of the big bison's head which hung upon the wall. They crossed the grinning skull of the gray wolf. They softened the eyes of the antelope's head, and made dark lines behind the long-tined antlers of the elk and of the deer. They brought forth to 140 view in alternate eclipse and definition the great, grim bear's head which hung above the mantel. Every trophy gathered in years of the chase, once perhaps prized, now perhaps forgotten, was brought into evidence, nor could one escape noting each one, and giving to each, for this one night more, the story which belonged to it. I sat and looked upon them all, and so there passed a panorama of the years.

"There," thought I, "is the stag which once fell far in the pine woods of the North. This antelope takes me back to the hard, white Plains. These huge antlers could grow only amid the forests of the Rockies. That wolf—how many of the hounds he mangled, I remember; and the giant bear, it was a good fight he made, perhaps dangerous, had the old rifle there been less sure. Yes, yes, of 141 course, I could recall each incident. Of course, they all were thrilling, exciting, delightful, glorious, all those things. Of course, the heart must have leaped in those days. The blood must have surged, in those moments. The pulse must have grown hard, the mouth must have been dry with the ardor of the chase, at those times. But now? But why? Does the heart leap to-night, do the veins fill with the rush of the blood, tumultuous in the joy of stimulus or danger? Why does not the old eagerness come back? Which of these trophies is the one to bring this back again? To which of these grim, silent heads belongs the keenest story?"

"I know," said the Singing Mouse, which unknown to me had come and placed itself upon the table. "I know." And it climbed upon my arm which lay across the table. The fire shone fair 142 upon its little form, so that in silhouette its outline was delicate and keen as an image cut from the fiery heart of a noble opal stone.

"And what is it that you know?" I asked. "Maker of dreams, tell me what you know to-night."

The Singing Mouse balanced and moved itself in harmony with the beat of the fire's rays. I looked at it so closely that a dream came upon my eyes, so that the voice of the Singing Mouse sounded far away and faint, though it was still clear and resonant in its own peculiar way and very fine and sweet.

"I will tell you which trophy you most prize," it said. "I will show you your *Iliad* of the chase. Do you not remember, do you not see this, the most eventful hunting of all your life?"

And so I gazed where the Singing 143 Mouse pointed, quite beyond the dusty walls, and there I saw as it had said. I heard not the thunder of the hoofs of buffalo, nor the faint crack of the twig beneath the panther's foot. I saw not the lurching gallop of the long-jawed wolf, nor the high, elastic bounding of the deer. The level swinging speed of the antelope, the slinking of the lynx, the crashing flight of the wapiti—no, it was none of these that came to mind; nor did the mountains nor the plains, nor the wilderness of the pines. But when the Singing Mouse whispered, "Do you see?" I murmured in reply, "I see it all again!"

I saw the small, low hills, well covered with short oaks and hazel bushes, which rolled on away from the village, far out, almost to the Delectable Mountains, which are well known to be upon the 144 edge of the world. Through these low hills a winding road led on, a road whose end no man had ever reached, but which went to places where, no doubt, many wonders were—perhaps even to the Delectable Mountains; for so a wise man once had said, his words harkened to with awe. This was a pleasant road, lined with brave sumacs, with bushes of the wild blackberry, and with small hazel trees which soon would offer fruit for the regular harvest of the fall, this same to be spread for drying on the woodshed roof. It was perhaps wise curiosity as to the crop of nuts which had brought thus far from home these two figures—an enormous distance, perhaps at least a mile beyond what heretofore had been the utmost limit of their wanderings. It was not, perhaps, safe to venture so far. There were known to be 145 strange creatures in these woods, one knew not what. It was therefore well that the younger boy should clasp tightly the hand of the older, him who bore with such confidence the bow and arrows, potent weapons of those days gone by!

It was half with fear and half with curiosity that these two wandered on, along this mysterious road, through this wild and unknown wilderness, so far from any habitation of mankind. The zeal of the explorer held them fast. They scarce dared fare farther on, but yet would not turn back. The noises of the woods thrilled them. The sudden clanging note of the jay near by caused them to stop, heart in mouth for the moment. Strange rustlings in the leaves made them cross the road, and step more quickly. Yet the cawing of a crow across the woods seemed friendly, and a small brown bird 146 which hopped ahead along the road was intimate and kind, and thus touched the founts of bravery in the two venturous hearts. Certainly they would go on. It was no matter about the sun. This was the valley of Ajalon, perhaps, of which one had heard in the class at Sabbath-school. And surely this was a good, droning, yellow-bodied bee—where did the bees go to when they rose up straight into the air? And this little mouse, what became of it in winter? And—ah! What was that—that awful burst of sound?

Clutch closer, little brother, though both be pale! How should either of you yet know the thunderous flight of the wild grouse, this great bird which whirled away through the brown leaves of the oaks? Father must be asked about this tremendous, startling bird. Meantime, the heart having begun to beat 147 again, let the two adventurers press yet a little farther on.

And so, with fears and tremblings, with doubts and joys, through briers and flowers, through hindrances and recompenses, along this crooked, winding, unknown road which led on out into the Unknown, they wandered, as in life we all are wandering to-day.

But hush! Listen! What is it, this sound, approaching, coming directly toward the road? Surely, it must be the footfall of some large animal, this cadenced rustling on the leaves! It comes — it will cross near — there, it has turned, it is near the road! Look! There it is, a great animal, half the length of one's arm, with bushy, long red tail arched high for easier running, its grayish coat showing in the bars of sunlight, its eyes bright and black and keen. Had it not 148 been said there were wild animals in these woods?

Each heart now thumped hard with the surging blood it bore; but it was now the blood of hunters and not of boys. Fear vanished at the sight of the quarry, and the only thought remaining was that of battle and of victory. Well for the animal that it ran — ill for it that it ran down the road and not back into the cover. The bow twanged, the arrow flew — blunt, but keenly sped. Down went the smitten prey! Pæan! Forward! Victory!

But ho! the creature rallies — recovers! It gathers its forces, it flies! Pursuit then, but pursuit apparently useless, for the animal has found refuge deep in this hollow stump, beyond the reach of longest mortal arm!

Rustle now, ye leaves, and threaten 149 now, all ye boughs with menacings. Roar, grouse, and clamor on, all ye jangling jays. No longer can ye strike terror into these two souls, small though they be. The heart of the hunter has now been born for each. Fear and defeat are known no longer in the compass of their thoughts. Follow, follow, follow! So spake the good old savagery of the natural man. Better for this creature had it never disturbed these two with its footfalls approaching among the leaves. Out of its refuge now must it come. Yea, though one lost a thousand suppers that night, and though a thousand stones lay waiting in the dark along the road to hurt bare, unprotected toes.

The sun forgot its part, and sank red, though reluctant, beyond the Delectable Mountains. Thou moon, this is Ajalon! Be kindly, for by moonlight one still may 150 labor, and here is labor to be done. Every blade in the Barlow knives is broken. The hole in the stump yields not to slashings, nor to attempts to pry it open. The prey is still unreached. What is to be done?

The elder hunter bethinks him of a solution for this problem. The broken blade will do to gnaw off this bough, and it will serve to make a split in the end of it. And if one be fortunate, and if this split

bestride the tail of the concealed animal, and if the stick be twisted —

"I've got him!" cried this philosopher for his "Eureka." And then
there was twisting and pulling, and scratching and squeaking, and
bitten fingers and tears; but after all was over, there lay the squirrel
vanquished, at the feet of these young barbarians who had wandered out from home into the unknown lands of earth. Cruel barbarians, thoughtless, 151 relentless! But how much has the world
changed?

The moon was over Ajalon when these two hunters, after all the
perils of the long, black road, marched up into the dooryard, bearing on a pole between them their quarry, well suspended by the
gambrels. "My boys, I feared that you were lost!" exclaims the tear-
ful mother who stands waiting in the door. But the silent father,
standing back of her in the glow of the lamplight, sees what the pole
is bearing, and in his eye there is a smile. After that, motherly re-
proach, fatherly inquiry, plenteous bread and milk, many eager
explanations and much descriptive narrative simultaneously ut-
tered by two mouths eager both to eat and to talk.

"I see it all," I said to the Singing Mouse. "It all comes back again.
No 152 chase was ever or will ever be so great as this one — back
there, near the Delectable Mountains, in those days gone by, those
incomparable days of youth! I thank you, Singing Mouse; but I beg
you do not go for yet a time. The heads upon the wall grin much,
and the dust lies thick upon them all."

155

157 Thumbnail

The Passing
of Men

One night the moon was shining brightly upon the curtain, which had been drawn tight across the window. Within the room the light was dim, so that there could be seen clearly the pictures which the moon was drawing on the curtain, figures which marched, advanced, receded. One might almost have thought these the shadows of some moving boughs, had one not known the ways the moon has at certain times.

It chanced that high up in the curtain there was a tiny hole, and through this opening the moonlight streamed, falling upon the table in a small, silvery ellipse, 158 of a size which one might cover ten times with one's hand. It was natural that in this little well of pale and dreamlike radiance the Singing Mouse should find it fit to manifest itself. I knew not when it came, but as I looked, the spot had found a tenant. The small, transparent paws of the Singing Mouse displayed no shadow as they waved and swung across this pencil of the pale, mysterious light. Yet its eyes shone opaline and brilliant as it sat, so that I could hardly gaze without a shiver of surprise akin to fear, fascinated as though I looked upon a thing unreal. Thus surrounded, almost one might say thus penetrated, by the translucent shaft of radiance which came through the window, the Singing Mouse told me of the figures on the curtain, which now began to have more distinct semblances.

159 "Do you see the figures there?" said the Singing Mouse. "Do you see the marching men? Have you never heard the hoofs ring on the roof when the wind blows high? Have you not seen their ranks sweep swift across the sky when storms arise? Have you never seen them marching through the long aisles of the wood at night? These are the warriors of the past. Now earth has always loved the warriors."

I looked, and indeed it was the truth. There was a panorama on the curtain. History had unrolled her scroll. The warriors of the nations and the times were passing.

I saw the men of Babylon, and those who came out of Egypt. Dark were these of hair and visage, and their arms were the ancient bow and spear. And there were those who rode light and cast 160 back their rapid archery. These faded, and in their stead marched men close-knit in solid phalanx, with long spears offering impenetrable front. In turn these passed away, and there came men with haughty brow, who bore short spears and swords. Near by these were wild, huge men of yellow hair, whose shields were leather and whose swords were broad and long. And as I gazed at all of these, my blood thrilling strangely at the sight, the figures blended and formed into a splendid procession of a martial day gone by. I saw them—a long stream of mounted men, who rode in helmet and cuirass, and bore each aloft a long-beamed spear. In front rode one whose mien was high and stern, and who might well have been commander. High aloft he tossed his great sword as he rode, and

sang the time a song of 161 war; and as he sang, the thousands of deep throats behind him made chorus terrible but stirring in its chesty melody, for ictus to the song each warrior smiting sword on shield in a mighty unison whose high, sonorous note thrilled like the voice of actual war. Steady the strong eyes gleamed out and onward as they rode. From the steel-clad breast of each there shone forward a glancing ray of light, as though it came direct from the heart, untamed even by a thousand years of death. My heart leaped to see them ride, so straight and stern and fearless, so goodly, so glorious to look upon. Came the rattle of chain, the clang of arms, the jangle of belt and spur; and still the brave procession passed, in tens, in hundreds, in thousands, in a long wave of stately men, whose eyes shone each in all the bold delight of 162 war. Stooped front, hooked hand and avaricious eye — these were as absent as the glow of gold or silver. It was the glorious age of steel.

Still on they passed, always arising the hoarse swell of the fighters' chorus. I heard the rumble of the many hoofs, thrilling even the impassive earth. The spear points shone. The harness rattled. The pennants fluttered stiffly in the breeze. And then afar I heard a sweet, compelling melody, the invitation of the bugle, that dearest mistress of the heart of man. My blood leaped. I started up. I started forward. The sweep of the ranks drew me on and in irresistibly. I would have raised my voice. I sought to stay, if for but one instant, this army of brave men, this panorama of exalted war, this incomparable pageant of a day 163 gone by! It was the Singing Mouse that checked me; for I heard it sigh:

"Alas!"

And yet again the scene was changed. Across the view streamed yet a long line of warriors. The hair of these did not float yellow from beneath loosened casque, nor indeed did these know aught of armor, nor did they march with banners beckoning, nor to the wooing of the trumpet's voice. The skins of these were red, and their hair was raven-black. Arms they had, and horses, though rude the one and ill-caparisoned the other. Leather and wood, and flint and sinew served them for material. Ill-armed they were; but as they rode, with naked breasts and painted faces, and tall feathers nodding in their plaited hair, out of the eye of each there shone the soul 164 of the fighting man, the warrior, beloved since ever earth began. Not less than the men of Babylon were these, nor than they of the ancient bow and spear, nor than they of the steel-clad breast; and as I saw them naked, clad only in the armor of a man's fearlessness, the word of commendation was as ready as that of pity.

"They are late, Singing Mouse," said I, "late in the day of war."

"Yes," said the Singing Mouse, with sadness, "they are late, and they must pass away. But they are warriors of proof, as much as any of those who have passed. Did you not see the melancholy of each face as it looked forward? Their fate was known, yet they rode forward to meet it fearlessly, as brave as any fighting men of all the years. In time, they too shall have their story, and with 165 the other warriors of the earth shall march again upon the page of history."

As I looked, the figures of these men grew dimmer. The tinkling of beaded garments and the shuffling of the ponies' hoofs became less and less distinct, and the dust cloud of their traveling became fainter and fainter, and finally faded and melted away. The curtain was bare. I heard the sighing of the wind.

167

169 Thumbnail

The House
of Truth

O

ne morning I lay upon my bed in the little room which I call my home. Now, among the eaves which rise opposite to my window there are many sparrows which have also made their homes. In the morning, before the sun has arisen, and at the time when the dawn is making the city gray and leaden in color instead of somber and black, these sparrows begin to chatter and chirp and sing in discordant notes, and by this I know the day has come. Upon this morning it seemed to me the sparrows chattered with an unusual commotion; and as I listened I heard from another window near mine the voice of 170 grief and lamentation. Then I knew that one who had long been sick had passed away. As the gray morning came on, this spirit, this spark of life, had gone out from its accustomed place. As the day came on, the sounds of lamentation arose. The friends of that one wept. So I asked the sparrows, and the sun, and the gray sky why these friends wept. What is grief? I asked of them. Why should these weep? What has happened when one dies? Where has the spark of life gone? Did it fall to these sodden pavements, for ever done, or did it go on up, to meet the kiss of the rising sun? And the sparrows, which fall to the ground, answered not. The sun rose calm and passionless, but dumb. The sky folded in, large but inscrutable. None the less arose the voice of lamentation and of woe.

171 "I ask you, Singing Mouse," said I, one night as we sat alone, "what is the Truth? How do we reach it? How shall we know it? Tell me of this spark that has gone out. Tell me, what is life, and where does it go? There are many words. Tell me, what is the Truth?"

The Singing Mouse gazed at me in its way of pity, so I knew I had asked that which could not be. Yet even as I saw this look appear it changed and vanished. And as the Singing Mouse waved its tiny paw I forbore reflection and looked only on the scene which now was spread before me. It seemed a picture of actual colors, and I could see it plainly.

I saw a youth who stood with one older and of austere garb. By the vestments of this older man I knew he was of those who teach people in spiritual things. To him the young man had come 172 in anguish of heart. Then the older man of priestly garb taught the young man in the teachings that had come down to him. But the youth bowed his head in trouble, nor was the cloud cleared upon his heart. I heard him murmur, "Alas! what is the Truth?"

So I saw this same youth pass on, in various stages of this picture, and before him I saw drawn, as though in another picture, a panorama of the edifices and institutions of the religions of all lands.

But the years passed, and the panorama of beliefs swept by, and no one could tell this man what was the Truth.

Yet after this young man had ceased to query and had closed his books, he one day entered alone into one of the great edifices built for the sake of that which he could not understand. In the picture I could see all this. I saw the young 173 man cast himself face down among the cushions of a seat, and there he lay and listened to the music. This, too, I could hear. I could hear the peal of the organ arise like voices of the spirits, going up, up, whispering, appealing, promising, assuring. Then—for I could see and hear with him— there came to that young man when he ceased to seek, the very exaltation he had longed to know.

"Ah! yes, Singing Mouse," I said, "it was very beautiful. But music is not final. Music is not the Truth. Tell me of these things."

The Singing Mouse again seemed to hesitate. "It may be," said the Singing Mouse slowly, "that the Truth will never be found between the covers of any book, no matter how wise. It may be that it never will be found by any who search 174 for it always within walls built by human hands. It may be that no man can convey to another that which is the Truth to him. It may be that the Truth can never be grasped, never be weighed or formulated.

"The ways of Nature are always the same, but Nature does not ask exactness of form. Why, then, shall we ask exactness of faith? The true faith is nothing final, not more than are final the carved stones of the church which offers it so strenuously. The stones crumble and decay, but new churches rise. New faiths will rise. But were not all well?"

At these things I wondered, and over them I thought for a time, but yet I did not understand all that the Singing Mouse had said. As if it knew my thought, the Singing Mouse said to me:

"Your vision is too narrow. You seek 175 the great truths in small places, and wonder that you do not find them. Come with me."

The Singing Mouse waved its hand, as was its wont, and as in a dream and as though I were now the young man whom we had lately seen, I was transported, by what means I could not tell, into a place far distant. At first it seemed to me there was a figure in vestments, speaking I scarce knew of what. Again there was a church or a cathedral. I could see the rafters as I lay. I could hear the solemn and exalted peal of the organ. I could hear voices that sang up and up, thrilling, compelling.

The sense of the confinement of the building ceased. Insensibly I seemed to see the hewn stones of the walls assume their primeval and untouched state beneath the grasses of the hills. I could feel 176 the rafters vanishing and going back into the bodies of the oaks in which they originally grew. The voice of the organ remained with me, but it might have been the roll of the waves upon the shore. I was in the Temple. In the Temple, one needs not seek for names.

It was night. I lay upon a bank of sweet-smelling grasses, and about me were the great oaks. The organ, or the waves, spoke on. I looked up, up, into the great circle of the sky, so far, so blue, so kind in its bending over, so pitying it seemed to me, yet so high in its up-reaching. I looked upon the glorious pageant of the stars.

"That star," thought I, "shone over the grave of some ancestor of mine; back, back in the unmirrored past, some father of some father of mine. He is gone, like a fly. He is dust. I may be 177 lying on his grave. Soon, like a fly, I, too, shall be dead, gone, turned into dust. But the star will still shine on. Small as that father's dust may be, that dust still lives. It is about me. This grass, these trees, may hold it. He has lived again in the cycle of natural forces. My dust, when I am dead, will in turn make part of this world, one of an unknown sea of stars. Small then, as I am, I am kin to that star. The stars go on. Nature goes on. Then shall man—shall I—"

"Ah," said the Singing Mouse, its voice sounding I knew not whence; "from this place can you see?"

So now I thought I began to see what I had not seen before. And since this was in the land of the Singing Mouse, I sought to find no name for what I saw, nor tried to measure it. What one man sees is not what another sees. Shall 178 one claim wisdom beyond his neighbor? Are not the stars his also, and the trees his, to talk with him? Are not the doors always open? Does not the music of the organ ever roll, do not the voices always rise?

Had it not been for the Singing Mouse I should not have thought these things.

181

183 Thumbnail

Where the
City Went

One day there was a white frost that fell upon the city, lasting for many hours, so that a strange thing happened, at which men wondered very much. The city put aside its colors of black and brown and gray, and dressed itself in silvery white. No stone nor brick was seen except in this silvern frosty color. All the spires were glittering in silver, and all the columns bore traceries as though the hands of spirits had labored long and delicately and had seen their tender fretwork frozen softly but for ever into silver. The gross city had put aside corporeal things, and for once its spirit shone fair and radiant; so that 184 men said no such thing had ever been before.

That evening the frost still remained, and as the night came on a mist fell upon the city. From the windows men looked out, and lo! the beautiful city so made spiritual was vanishing. One by one the great buildings, the tall spires, the lofty columns had faded into a white dream, dimmer, fainter, less and less perceptible, seen through a gentle envelope of whitening haze. This thing was of a sort almost to make one tremble as he looked upon it, for the city which had been silver had turned to mist, and the mist seemed fair to turn into a dream. There are those who say it did become a dream, and afterward descended. For wanderers in desert countries tell that at times they have seen some far city of 185 dreams, alluringly beautiful, but evanescent, intangible, unattainable, trembling and floating upon the wavering air.

Now when I saw the city thus fade away and disappear, I sat down at my table, and, as many men did that night, I wondered much at what I had seen. For surely the soul of the city had arisen. Then the Singing Mouse came and gazed into my face.

"What you have seen is true," said the Singing Mouse. "There is no city now. It has gone. You have seen it disappear. Its soul has arisen. This does not often happen, yet it can be, for even the city has a soul if you can find it.

"But if I say the city has gone, I mean only that it has left the place where once it was. That which once was, is always, corporate or not corporate. We err only 186 when we ask to see all with our eyes, to balance all within our hands. Come with me, and I will show you where the city went."

So now the Singing Mouse waved its hands, and I saw, though I knew not where I looked.

I saw a country where the trees grew big and where the wild-fowl came. It was where the trees had never been felled, nor had the stones ever been hewn. The sky was blue, and the water was blue, except where it played and laughed, and there it was white.

There was a small house, of a sort one has never seen, for none in the cities is like it. The blue smoke curling from the chimney named it none the less a home. I hardly knew what time or place we had come upon, for the Singing Mouse, whose voice seemed high and 187 exalted, spoke as though much was in the past.

"This is a Home," said the Singing Mouse. "Once there were no homes. In those days there was only one fire, and it was red. By this man sat. He sought not to see.

"Once a man sat at night and looked up at the heavens, seeking to know what the stars were saying. He besought the stars, praying to them and asking them to listen to the voice of the water, and to the voice of the oaks and to the whispers of the grasses, and to tell him why the fire of earth was red, while the fire of the stars was white.

"Now, while this man besought the stars, to him a strange thing happened. As he looked up he saw falling from the heavens above him a ray of the white light of the stars. It fell near to him 188 and lay shining like a jewel in the grass. To this the man ran at once, gladly, and took up the white light, and put it in his bosom, that the winds might not harm it. Always this man kept the white light in his bosom after that. And by its light he saw many things which till that time men had never known. This man found that this new light, with the red light that had been known, filled all his house with a great radiance, so that small strifes were not so many, and so that life became plain and sweet. This then that you see is that Home.

"This that you see around you," it continued slowly, "the large trees and the green grass, and the blue sky and the smiling waters, all this is wealth; wealth not corporate, wealth valuable, wealth that belongs to every man ever born upon the earth, and which can not of 189 right ever be taken away from him. Shorn of that, he is poor indeed, though not so poor as he who shore him. Unshorn of this, he is rich. In our land our hearts ache to see these terms misused, and that called wealth which is so far from worth the having. But here, where I have brought you, you shall see humanity undwarfed, and you shall see peace and largeness in the life which you once thought small and sordid."

Then as I looked, there stepped from the house a man, or one whom I took to be a man. This man stood in the cool, fresh morning, and gazed at the sun, now rising above the tops of the great trees. He smiled gently, and taking in each hand a little water from a tiny stream that flowed near by, he raised his hands, and still smiling, offered tribute of the water to the sun. I saw the water falling 190 down from his hands in a small stream of silver drops, shining brightly. It was the way of the land, the Singing Mouse said; for they thought that as the water came from the sky and returned to it, so did man and the thoughts of man, and the fruits of his progress; never to be destroyed.

At all this I looked almost in fear, for the thought came that perhaps this was not Man as we knew him, but the successor of Man. "Where is this land," I asked of the Singing Mouse, "and what is this time upon which we have come?"

The Singing Mouse looked at the green trees, and at the kind sun, and at the blue sky and the pleasant waters, and it said to me slowly: "There was once a city where these trees now stand."

193

195 Thumbnail

The Bell and
the Shadows

Melody unformulate, music immaterial, such was the voice of the Singing Mouse; faint, small and clear, a piping of fifes so fine, a touching of strings so delicate, that it seemed to come from instruments of beryl and of diamond, a phantom music, impossible to fetter with staff or bar, and past the hope of compassing in words.

It was the last night of the year, and the bell upon the church near by had made many strokes the last time it had been heard; many heavy strokes which throbbed sullenly, mournfully on the air. The presence of passing Time was at hand. The year soon would join the 196 years gone by. Regret, remorse, despair, abandonment, the hopelessness of humanity—was it the breath of these which arose and burdened heavily the note of the chronicling bell? Where were the chimes of joy?

"These shadows that you see are not upon the wall," said the Singing Mouse. "They are very much beyond the windows. If only we will look out from our windows, there are always great pictures waiting for us—pictures in pearl and opal, in liquid argent, in crimson and gold. But always there must be the shadows. Without these, there can be no picture anywhere.

"Have you not seen what the shadows do? Have you not seen them trooping through the oak forest in the evening, through the pine forest in open day, 197 across the prairies under the moon at night, legions of them, armies of them? Have you never seen them march across the grass-lands in the daytime, cohort after cohort, hurrying to the call of the unseen trumpets? In the woods, have you never heard strange sounds, when you put your ear to the ground—sounds untraceable to any animate life? Have you never heard vague voices in the trees? Have you not heard distant, mysterious noises in the forest, whose cause you could never learn, seek no matter how you might? These were the voices of the shadows, the people who live there. Who else should it be to whisper and sing to you and make you happy when you are there? Without these people, what would be the woods, the prairies, the waters, the sky, the world?

"Without the shadows, too, what 198 would be our lives? Thoughts, thoughts and remembrances, what have we that is sweeter than these? Have you never seen the smile upon the lips of those who have died? They say they are looking upon the Future. Perhaps they look also upon the Past, and therefore smile in happiness, seeing again Youth, and Hope, and Faith, and Trust; which are tender and beautiful things. Life has no actuality of its own, and in material sense is only a continual change. But the shadows of thought and of remembrance do not change. It is only the shadows that are real."

As I pondered upon this, there passed by many pleasant pictures upon the wall, after the way the Singing Mouse had; many pictures of days gone by, which made me think that perhaps what the Singing Mouse had said was true.

199 I could see the boy, sitting idle and a-dream, watching the shadows drifting across the clover fields where the big bees came. I saw the youth wandering in the woods where the squirrels lived, loitering and looking, peering into corners full of the secrets of the wild creatures, unraveling the delicious mysteries which Nature ever offers to those not yet grown old. It was a comfortable picture, full of the brilliant greens of springtime, the mellow tints of summer, the red and russet of autumn days, the blue and white of winter. I could hear, also, sounds intimately associated with the scenes before me; the bleat of little lambs, the low of cattle, the neighing of a distant horse.

And then both sound and scene progressed, and once more as the woods and hills grew bolder and more wild, I 200 could hear clearly the rifle's thin report, could note the whisper of the secret-loving paddle, the slipping of the snow-shoe on the snow, the clatter of the hoofs of horses, the baying of the bell-mouthed hounds. The delights of it all came back again, and in this varied phantom chase among the keen joys of the past, I saw as plainly and exultantly as ever in my life, the panorama of the brown woods, and the gray plains, and the purple hills—saw it distinctly, with all the old vibrant joy of youth—line for line, sound for sound, shadow for shadow, joy for joy!

And then the Singing Mouse, without wish of mine, caused these scenes to change into others of more quiet sort, which told not of the fields, but of the home. In the shadows of evening, I seemed to see a pleasant place, well surrounded by trees and flowers, the leaves 201 of which were stirred softly in the breath of a faint summer breeze, strong enough only to carry aloft in its hands the odor of the blooming rose. This picture faded slowly. There were shadows in the spaces between the trees. There were shadows in the dark-growing vine which draped a column. One could only guess if he caught sight of garb or of the outline of a form among the shadows. He could only guess, too, whether he heard music, faint as the breeze, faint as the incense of the flowers. He could only guess if he had seen the image of the House Beautiful, that temple known as Home.

"Thoughts," said the Singing Mouse softly. "Thoughts and remembrances. These are the things that live for ever. It is only the shadows that are real!"

202 The solemn note of the bell struck in. It counted twelve. The new year had come. The chimes of joy arose. But still the faint music from the Past had not died away, and still the shadows waved and beckoned on the wall, strong and beautiful, and enduring, and not like the fading of a dream. So then I knew that what the Singing Mouse had said was true, and that it is, indeed, only the shadows that are real.

205

Of the Greatest Sorrow...

Of the Greatest
Sorrow

A

thousand times in the night I reach out (it seems to me), and touch her hair as it lies spread and dark. A thousand times in the night I gaze upon her face, her eyes shielded, her lips gently closed and curved. A thousand times in the night (it seems to me), I bend above her and whisper, "I love you!" And she, though asleep and myriads of miles away among the stars, hears me always and stirs just faintly, and still sleeping whispers through lips that barely part, "I know!" It is perhaps that thing called Love which causes me to do this, because I always whisper, "I love you;" though no word quite is 208 wide and deep and soft and kind enough to say what is in the soul at certain times.

Now in lives there are ways. Some have few sorrows and many things of fortune taken lightly, the things wished coming easily. Again, others gain only by pain and suffering and long effort and hard denyings. As it is decreed by chance, the way with most is to gain all things hardly, and to know always denial, and always to have longing. That is the way with most. Of these things I spoke with the Singing Mouse, and told of many things that came as sorrows and griefs and denials, saying that, since this was decreed by chance, there was naught that a man ought not to receive without murmur; and the Singing Mouse said that this was true, that many things were denied, and that many knew great sorrows. 209 This was the reason we came to speak of sorrows. I named very many sorrows that I had known, and many that friends of mine had known, some of these far greater than my own; as is most often the case when one comes to see deeply into these things.

"All sorrows," said the Singing Mouse, "come to us, and we must bear them, though some are very hard to bear; as when friends do not know we love them, and think us ill-formed and crooked, small and mean, when in truth in soul we are tall and comely, large and strong. Or when we are thought to have done a bad action when in truth we have done a good one; or when hunger and thirst come and we have little comforts; or when sickness and weakness come to us when we wish our strength; or when those die whom we have loved. All, all 210 these sorrows, and very many others, come to us; and each sorrow must be borne, for that is the way of life."

"What," I asked of the Singing Mouse, "is the greatest sorrow?"

"That," said the Singing Mouse, "is a thing hard to tell; for each man thinks that the sorrow that he has is the greatest sorrow for him or for the world; though perhaps in truth it is not large. What to you," asked the Singing Mouse, "is the greatest sorrow of those which have not yet come to you?"

... "A thousand times in the night, Singing Mouse," said I, "I reach out and touch her hair, as it lies spread and dark. I whisper to her, though she be myriads of miles away among the stars; and she hears; and she answers! This is because of that thing called Love. Now, this sorrow has not yet come to me; that when 211 I reach out my hand in the night I shall not touch her hair; that when I bend to kiss her sleeping she shall not be there any more; that when I whisper to her she may no longer answer to me, seeing that this thing called Love can be no more between us. That," said I to the Singing Mouse, "I could not endure."

Indeed, at the thought of this, so sharp an agony came to me that I arose and cried out loud. "I can not endure it, I can not endure it!" I cried (although this sorrow had not yet come to me).

"Ah!" said the Singing Mouse, "how idle and weak is the human mind in the country where you live. Have you not said but now that, though she be myriads of miles away among the stars, she answers you when you whisper? Does she not hear? Do not her lips move in speech as you whisper?"

212 "That is true," said I. "And will she always hear?"

"She will always hear," said the Singing Mouse. "So this sorrow will not come as you fear."

"And shall I reach out and touch her hair as it lies spread and dark?" This I asked of the Singing Mouse.

"You shall touch it, spread and dark, and fragrant as when you were young," said the Singing Mouse, "if so you wish."

So then it seemed that perhaps all sorrows, even very great ones, are a part of life. Although I know that, if I could no longer know the fragrance of her hair, or hear the whisper of her answer, then that sorrow would be more than I could bear.

215

217 Thumbnail

The Shoes of the Princess

Once I was in a place where there were those who had opened many tombs, and had taken from the tombs, that had been in Egypt, and were very old, many things that had been placed there for silence and repose thousands of years ago. There were grave-clothes and grave-caskets, the one embroidered, the other graven; and the colors of both were as they were thousands of years ago. There were signs over which men pondered, not knowing their own writing, and their own thoughts, and their own fate. There were also, a sad thing to see, the bodies of those that had died long ago, that had lain down for rest 218 and silence; and of these some were called kings, and some were called queens and others princesses; and all had once been young, and some had once been beautiful. For here, after thousands of years, was praise of their beauty, and love and care for it. So I pondered very long and sadly. But most I looked at two little golden shoes.

These little shoes had once been the shoes of one who lay here, a princess, dead thousands of years, and once very beautiful, as these carven symbols told. They were small and dainty and threaded with fine gold, and laced across with care about the feet of her who was once a woman and a princess and owner of much beauty, and who was in her life beloved, and in her death mourned; as these graven symbols said. A thousand years this love reached out its arms to 219 her to-day; although for a thousand years Death had enfolded her in his grasp, that does not yield. She who had lain down for rest and silence was still here, withal at rest in her grave-garb, and silent in her sleep; but those who had done these things had removed the grave-clothing so that these small shoes could be seen, still upon the feet of the princess that had slept a thousand years, enfolded in love.

For a price these might have sold the shoes of the princess, for there were those cruel enough to strip her of that which she had worn when she lay down to be alone. But this I could not do. I did not carry away the shoes in my hands, but in some way it seemed to me that I took them; for that night, as I sat at the little table in my room, with the dim light falling as is its wont at those hours, I saw upon the table before me 220 these same shoes of the princess of thousands of years ago, small and golden; things to make one weep, so sad their story, disturbed thus after they had been placed away for silence. I gazed at them for a time, and presently I saw appear upon the table beside them, the form of the Singing Mouse, as tall perhaps as the fronts of these golden shoes.

"See," said the Singing Mouse, "here are her shoes, those of the princess who has been resting. They crossed the paved floors of palaces. They knew the steps of a throne. They were made by love for love and given in love to rest and silence. She was as one you have known, as many whom others know now. Tell me, is she not beautiful?"

I saw standing before me the figure of the princess, tall and slender and very beautiful. And now the grave garments 221 were not seen, for her robe was of silk, new and soft and shapely like to herself, and her arms were round and soft, and her eyes were full and dark, and her hair was as deep shadows. A band of gold was about her brow, and her cheek was red and tender in its bloom. Her neck was white and round, and her hands were white, and her slender fingers curved slightly as her arms hung down by her sides. Her feet were small and straight, and all, all of her was beautiful, and she was a princess.

Now as I gazed, I saw the face and saw that it was one I knew, and had known long; so then I knew that the princess who was placed away for rest and silence had never died; for did she not stand here before me, and had I not long known her thus? Ah, beautiful!

I took up these small golden shoes in 222 my hands and held them out to her. "Take these little shoes," I said, "wrought as cunning as man may know. Place them upon thy feet for me, and may never thorn assail thee in all thy going. Wear them and tread the steps of thrones, years and years, ages and ages, Princess, beloved! See, they are wrought in love."

Now I saw upon the lips of the princess who had lain down thousands of years ago, but who lives in a place I know to-day, a smile, very faint and far away. So as the Singing Mouse told me, it was to be seen that she did not die. Even as she faded away from the wall against which she stood, I knew, though I wept, that the princess was not dead and would not die. She was beautiful, she was beloved; and these things have not died. "Ah, beautiful!" I said to the 223 Singing Mouse. "But alas! for a princess there should be a palace, and here is none!"

"Look about you," said the Singing Mouse. "See, for the time this is a palace."

I looked about me, and it was as the Singing Mouse said. For the time my room was a palace. I saw standing there again the princess, upon her feet small golden shoes.

"What is this?" I asked. "And who am I?" But as I turned, I saw that the Singing Mouse was gone. But this I knew, and so may you know: that love does not die; and here was proof of it.

225

227 Thumbnail

Of White

Moths

"Once," said the Singing Mouse, "I was at the side of a little stream. Grasses grew all about, and small plants and flowers. Beyond the shores of the little stream arose a forest, wide and dark, into which the eye could reach but a little way.

"As I stood near the little stream, there arose from the grass and flowers two small moths, soft and dainty, beautiful, and very white, covered also with a white dust or powder which was so light that did they but receive a touch they must lose some of this soft white powder 228 and so be injured, so gentle and tender were they.

"These two moths, soft and white and silent, arose in the air and circled one about the other, rising for a time, then falling, but ever circling one about the other. It seemed that perhaps they spoke one to the other, but if that were true it was in speech so small that not even I could hear it. They passed over the tops of the grasses and flowers, up and up, until they reached the tops of the trees, where they seemed very small.

"I do not know why these moths no longer cared for the grasses and flowers. But I saw them, circling, cross over the little stream, high in the air, and then pass on directly into the wide dark forest. For a moment they appeared, a small spot of white, against the black shadows of the forest across the stream; then they went 229 on, straight into the shadows, until I could no longer see this small spot of white they made.

"It is in this way," said the Singing Mouse, "that human souls pass through life. To me, who can see them, they look small and delicate and white; and they circle one about another; and they pass on, into the deep forest."

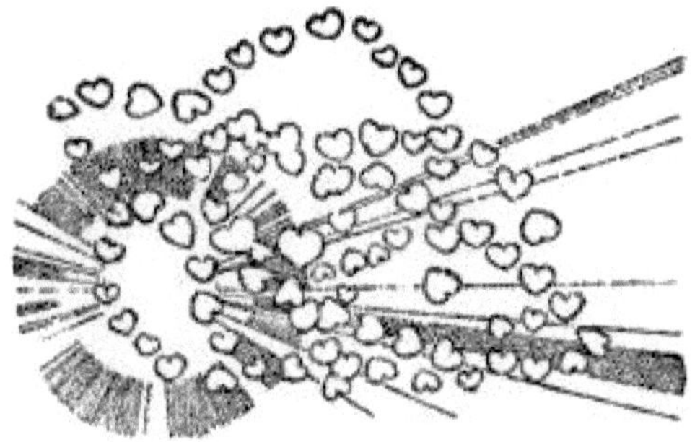

231

233 Thumbnail

The House
of Dreams

"U

pon what couch," I asked the Singing Mouse, "may one have the most noble dreams?"

The Singing Mouse sat for a time and looked at me with its bright eye, and it seemed to me that the walls opened and widened. I saw that I was within a great palace, whose walls were hung in tapestries, and whose doors were of golden panelings, and whose windows were of curious crystals, and whose furnishings were rich and wonderful, and around whose stately limits swam wide gardens of strange flowers, full of deep perfumes. I heard soft voices of birds 234 and the music also of gentle human voices singing, and tenderly played instruments of silken and silvern strings. It seemed to me that I lay upon a great couch of thrice-piled down, and touched hands with delights in all manners that one could think. But alas! I did not dream as I lay upon this couch.

Then I saw these walls fade away in turn, and in their stead arose a vast cathedral of the woods. A music was in the trees, and a solemn mountain stood as orator to the sky for me. My couch was that of the earth and the leaves, and my jewels were upon the grasses all about. I touched hands with delights; and so I dreamed, and was very happy and content.

Again the place changed, and I lay in my own small room, with naked walls and little cheer or comfort, as you may 235 see. The couch was hard and narrow, and that which covered it over was worn and threadbare, and by no means cloth of woven silk and golden tracery. But it seemed to me that upon the walls were pictures. And here and there were shadows of things which I had wished—many things, very sweet and precious. Upon this couch, as upon that of the earth, it seemed to me that I dreamed....

"There were once some leaves and grasses in this couch," said the Singing Mouse, "and that is why you dreamed. Around this manner of resting-place often arises the House of Dreams, and not, as many have supposed, about the couch of down and silken tapestries. Always, near a House of Dreams, must be a mountain or a sea, and trees, and grasses, with the sky also, and the stars, which are the candles of our dream 236 houses. See, you had not noticed it, but there is a star in your candle."

I looked, and it was as the Singing Mouse had said. A star was at the candle top. By its light I could dream nobly, and many things seemed true which have not yet come true when the star in the candle does not shine. But they are true in the land of the Singing Mouse. In that country it is not palaces alone that are Houses of Dreams. I know this thing is true. Wherefore, all ye who have come hither, let your hope and your joy be strong; and by no means despair, for better than despair are hope and joy.

Thumbnails

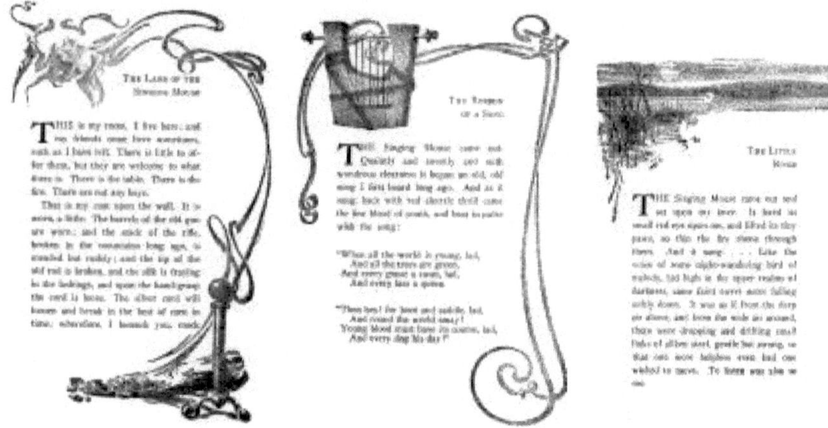

The Land of the Singing Mouse

The Burden of a Song

The Little River

What the Waters Said

Lake Belle-Marie

The Skull and the Rose

The Man of the Mountain   At the Place of the Oaks   The Birth of the Hours

The Tear and the Smile   How the Mountains Ate Up the Plains   The Savage and Its Heart

The Beast Terrible

The Passing of Men

The House of Truth

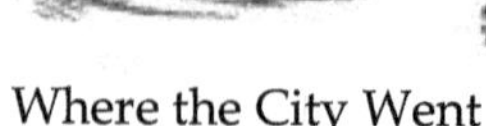

Where the City Went

The Bell and the Shadows

Of the Greatest Sorrow

The Shoes of the Princess   Of White Moths

The House of Dreams